Walt Disney's

The Aristocats

Senior Designer: Elaine Lopez
Editor: Sharon Fass Yates
Editorial Director: Pamela Pia

Walt Disney's The Aristocats copyright © 1970, 2005 Disney Enterprises, Inc.
The Aristocats is based on the book by Thomas Rowe. Illustrations by The Walt Disney Studios.

Copyright ©2008 Disney Enterprises, Inc. All Rights Reserved.
Published by Reader's Digest Children's Books,
Reader's Digest Road, Pleasantville, NY U.S.A. 10570-7000
and Reader's Digest Children's Publishing Limited,
The Ice House, 124-126 Walcot Street, Bath UK BA1 5BG
Reader's Digest Children's Books, the Pegasus logo,
and Reader's Digest are all registered trademarks of
The Reader's Digest Association, Inc. Manufactured in China.
1 3 5 7 9 10 8 6 4 2

Walt Disney's
The Aristocats

Illustrations by The Walt Disney Studios

Based on the book by Thomas Rowe

Reader's Digest Children's Books™

Pleasantville, New York • Montréal, Québec • Bath, United Kingdom

*I*n Madame Bonfamille's fine home in Paris, all was peaceful. Well, almost . . . .

"Me first!" Kitten Marie shouted. "I'm a lady!"

"Ha! You're not a lady," said her brother Toulouse.

"You're just a sister," said Berlioz.

"I'll show you!" Marie shouted.

Marie started after her brothers. A chase began that brought giggles and then tears, as Marie's tail somehow arrived in Berlioz's mouth.

"Children!" said Duchess, their mother.

"I was just practicing my biting, Mamma," said Berlioz.

"Aristocats do not bite," said Duchess. "Come, let's practice being ladies and gentlemen."

Soon all was peaceful again—but not for long. Out in the kitchen, someone was planning to do something bad to the Aristocats.

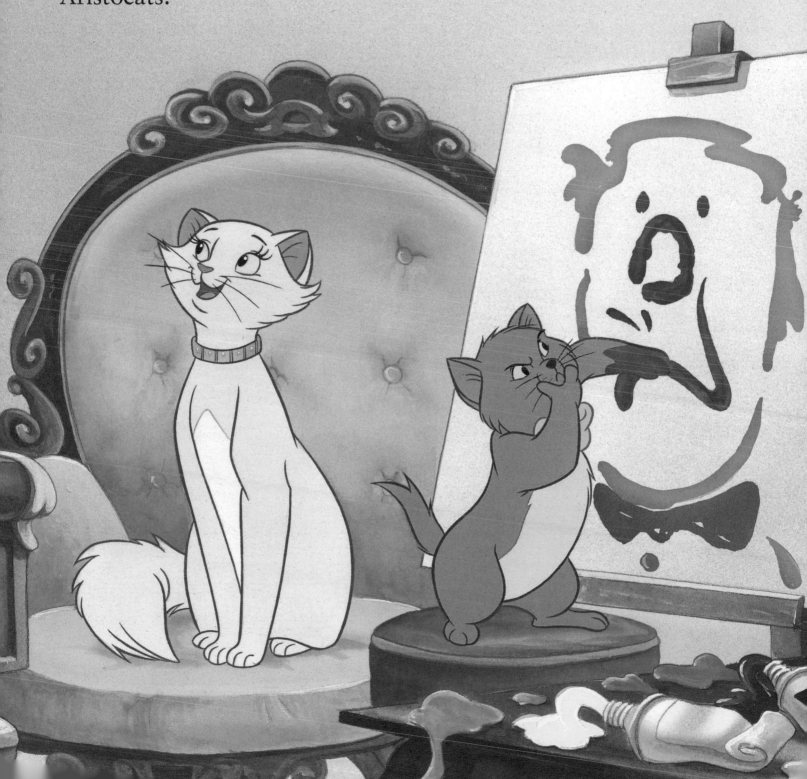

Edgar the butler had heard Madame say, "I'm leaving my fortune to my dear cats. Edgar may have what's left when they're gone."

Edgar had thought, "Four cats. Nine lives each. Four times nine is . . . is . . . too long. They'll outlive me, unless . . . ."

And, right then and there, Edgar planned a way to make the Aristocats disappear.

"Come, kitties," he called. "Come taste this delicious *crème de la Edgar*."

It *was* delicious. Their friend Roquefort the mouse thought so, too. But . . . everyone who drank it fell asleep!

And the Aristocats slept *so* soundly that they didn't know they left home in a basket on Edgar's motorcycle.

They didn't know that Edgar was chased by dogs, and that the basket fell off and landed under a bridge.

They didn't know they were alone, far out in the country, until a storm broke and they woke up.

"Mamma!" Marie called out. "I'm afraid!" Where are we?"

"I don't know, darling. I . . . I . . . Let's just try to sleep until morning."

But Duchess couldn't sleep. All she could do was worry.

Then she heard a rough voice singing, "I'm O'Malley the Alley Cat. Helpin' ladies is my—"

"Oh, Mr. O'Malley, can you help me?" Duchess called. "I'm in great trouble. I'm lost."

O'Malley bowed. "Yer ladyship, I'll fly you off on my magic carpet for two."

Berlioz popped up. So did Toulouse. And Marie. "What magic carpet?" they asked.

"Uh . . . er . . ." O'Malley stammered. Then he grinned. "Look, I said magic carpet for two, but it can be a magic carpet for *five* also." He made an X on the road. "It'll stop for passengers right here. Watch!"

They watched. Something came down the road. O'Malley made himself big and scary-looking and jumped out in front of it. The something stopped right on the X.

"All aboard!" said O'Malley. "One magic carpet, ready to go."

"Aw, it's just a truck," said Berlioz.

"Shh!" said Duchess. Then she smiled at O'Malley. "It's a lovely magic carpet. Is it going to Paris?" she asked.

"It's goin' somewhere," said O'Malley, helping her on.

But soon the driver of the magic carpet saw that he had passengers. He stopped with a jerk. He threw things. His passengers jumped to safety.

"What an awful man!" said Duchess. "I wish we were home."

"Humans are like that," said O'Malley.

"Oh, no, Mr. O'Malley," said Duchess. "*My* humans aren't like that."

"Hmm!" said O'Malley. "Then how did you get here? Somebody doesn't like you."

Duchess thought about that as they began the long walk back to Paris.

Finally they arrived in the city, so tired they could hardly take a step.

"We'll stop and rest at my peaceful pad," O'Malley said.

But the peaceful pad was bouncing with sound. "Oh . . . uh . . . friends have stopped by," O'Malley explained. "We'll go somewhere—"

"I'd like to meet your friends, Mr. O'Malley," said Duchess.

So O'Malley introduced all his swinging musician friends. What fun it was! They played for the four Aristocats, and Duchess sang for them.

Then, after the children were tucked in, Duchess and O'Malley talked.

"Your friends are delightful," said Duchess.

"How about sharin' them?" asked Mr. O'Malley. "I mean, how about stayin' here with me? Like forever."

Marie heard him. She whispered, "Mr. O'Malley's going to be our father . . . maybe."

"Great!" said Toulouse.

"Shhh!" said Marie. "Listen!"

"Oh, if I only could!" said Duchess. "But I can never leave Madame."

"She's lucky," said O'Malley. "I never felt that way about a human, and no human ever felt that way about me." He sighed. "But . . . well, I'll take you home."

The next day, O'Malley watched as Edgar opened the door for the Aristocats.

"Oh!" said Edgar. "You're back! I mean . . . uh, how *nice* to see you back!"

"Looks like they don't need me anymore," said O'Malley. He turned away sadly.

But O'Malley was wrong. The first thing Edgar did was put Duchess and her children into a bag. Then, when he heard Madame call, "Are my little dears back? Did I hear them?" Edgar popped the bag of cats into the nearest container and went to answer Madame's call.

The four Aristocats were stiff with fear. What would happen to them now? Then Duchess remembered Roquefort the mouse.

"Get O'Malley!" she called. She told him how to find her friend. "Hurry!"

Roquefort ran out, just as Edgar came back in with a trunk.

"Now," Edgar said, "you're going in this trunk to Timbuktu and *never* coming back! Onto the baggage truck you go and away forever." He opened the door.

But suddenly alley cats were everywhere. Two unlocked the trunk and let out the Aristocats.

And some, with a little help, put Edgar inside. Now someone else was on his way to Timbuktu!

And there were some happy cats who were very glad to stay home. Listen! You can hear a rough voice, and a lovely soft voice, and three little voices singing, . . .

"We're Mr. and Mrs. O'Malley. We're the *five* Aristocats."